THE MONSTER TRAP

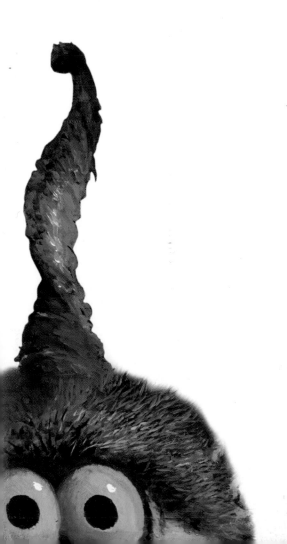

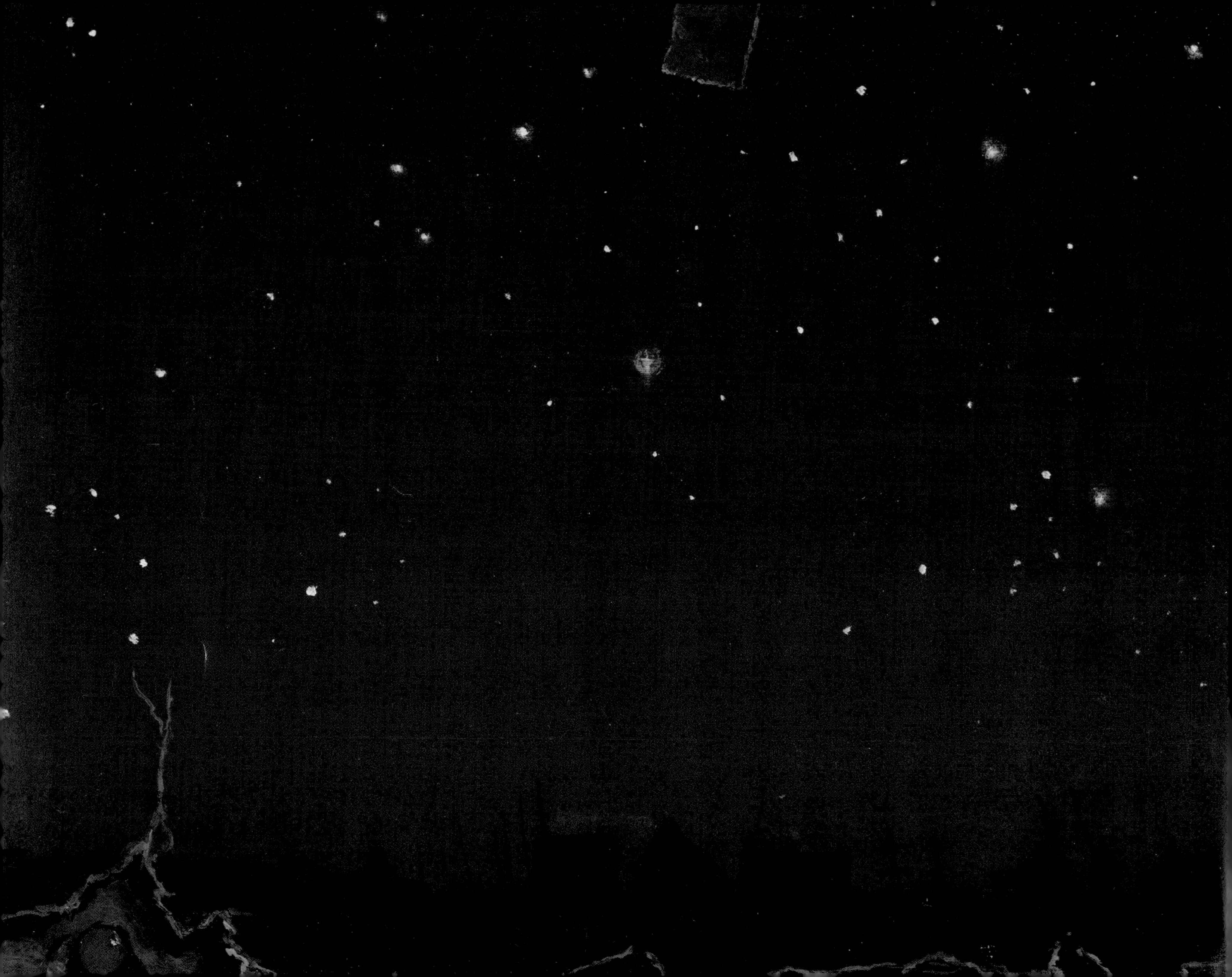

THE MONSTER TRAP

STORY AND PICTURES BY DEAN MORRISSEY

WRITTEN BY DEAN MORRISSEY AND STEPHEN KRENSKY

HARPERCOLLINSPUBLISHERS

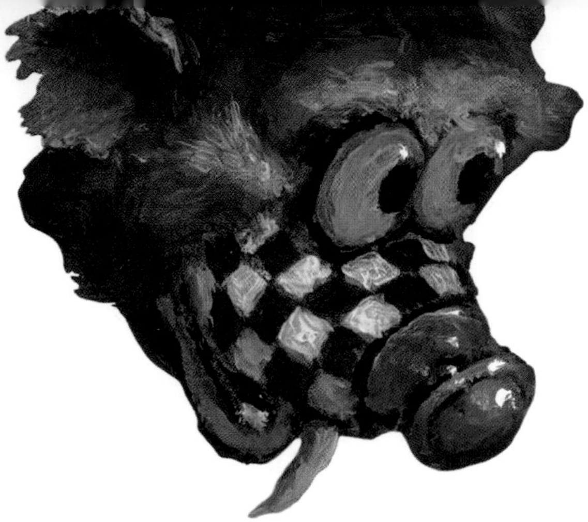

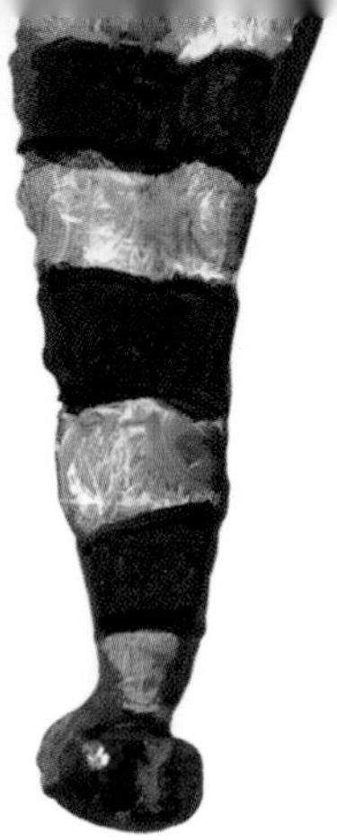

The Monster Trap

Story and pictures by Dean Morrissey
Written by Dean Morrissey and Stephen Krensky
Manufactured in China by South China Printing Company Ltd.
For information address HarperCollins Children's Books, a division of HarperCollins Publishers, 1350 Avenue of the Americas, New York, NY 10019.
www.harperchildrens.com

Library of Congress Cataloging-in-Publication Data
Morrissey, Dean.
The monster trap / story and pictures by Dean Morrissey ; written by Dean Morrissey and Stephen Krensky.
p. cm.
Summary: While visiting his grandfather, Paddy hears a story about monsters on the radio and is sure they are coming to the house to get him, but Pop has an idea sure to stop them—or will it?
ISBN 0-06-052498-7 — ISBN 0-06-052499-5 (lib. bdg.)
[1. Monsters—Fiction. 2. Grandfathers—Fiction. 3. Sleepovers—Fiction. 4. Fear of the dark—Fiction.]
I. Krensky, Stephen. II. Title.
PZ7.K883Mo 2004 2002008340
[Fic]—dc21

Typography by Al Cetta
1 2 3 4 5 6 7 8 9 10
❖
First Edition

This book is dedicated to the twenty-five kids I met with who had actually seen monsters of some sort with their own eyes. Their vivid descriptions and drawings are part of the fabric of this story.

–D.M.

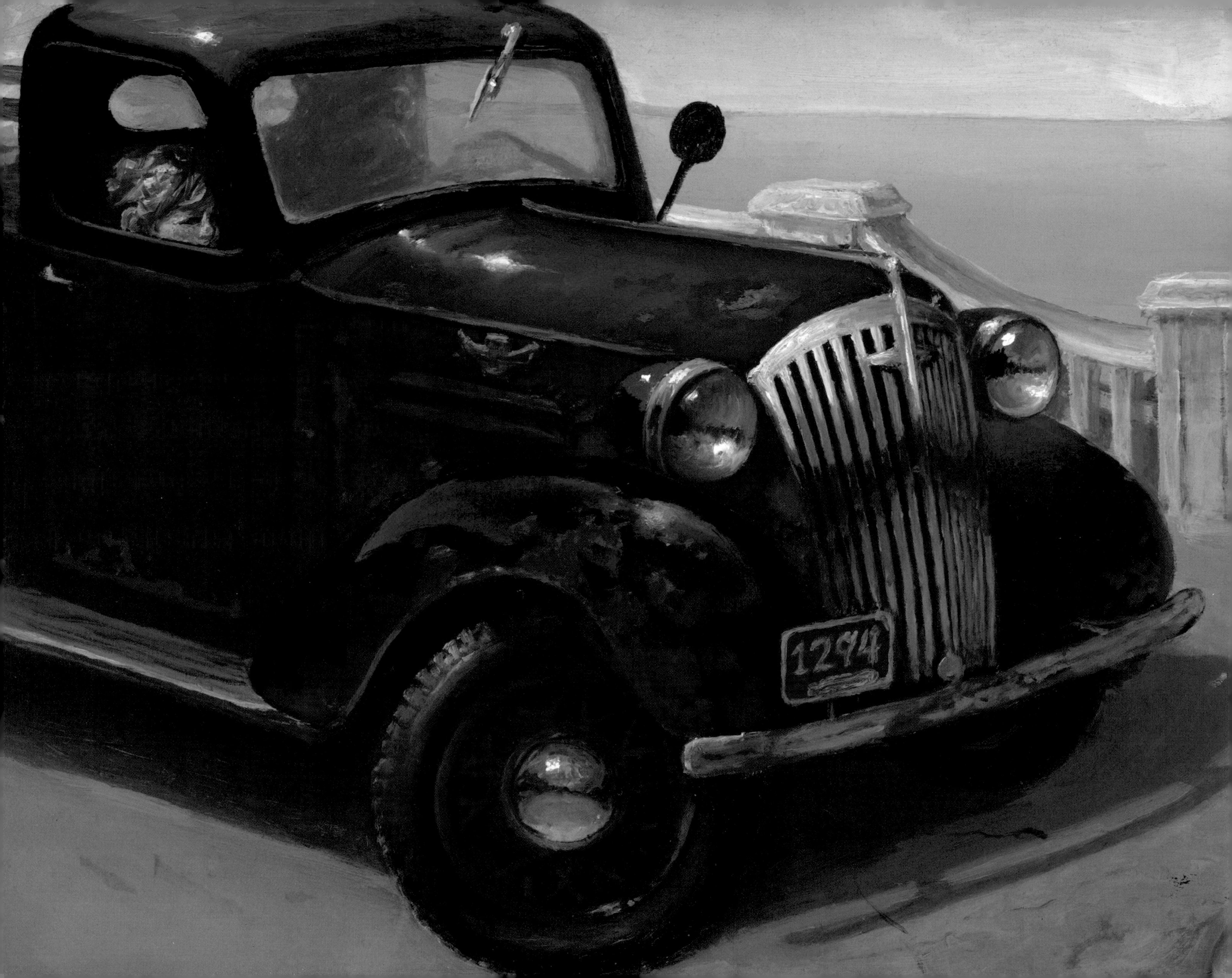
1294

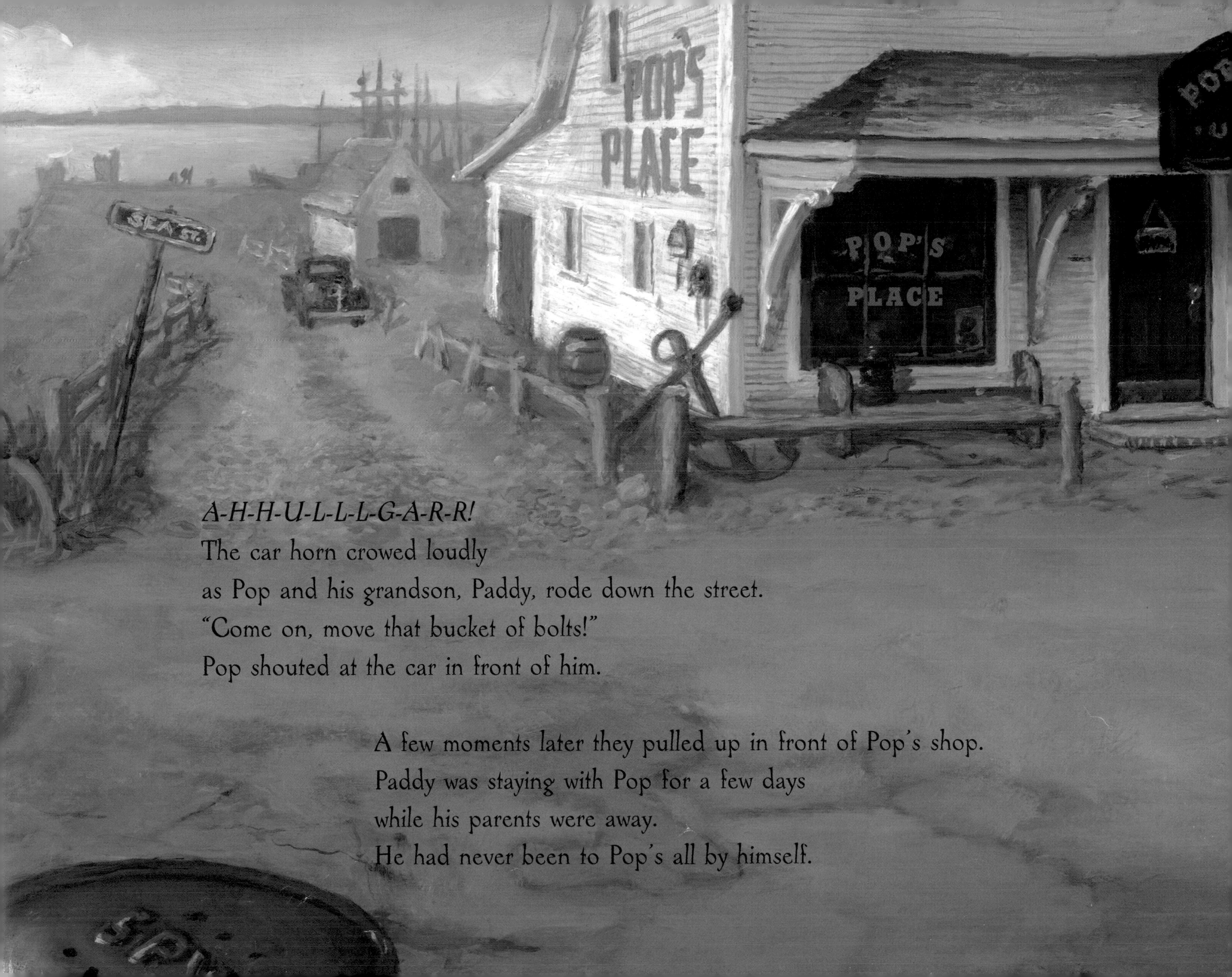
POP'S
PLACE
SEA ST.
POP'S
PLACE

A-H-H-U-L-L-L-G-A-R-R!
The car horn crowed loudly
as Pop and his grandson, Paddy, rode down the street.
"Come on, move that bucket of bolts!"
Pop shouted at the car in front of him.

A few moments later they pulled up in front of Pop's shop.
Paddy was staying with Pop for a few days
while his parents were away.
He had never been to Pop's all by himself.

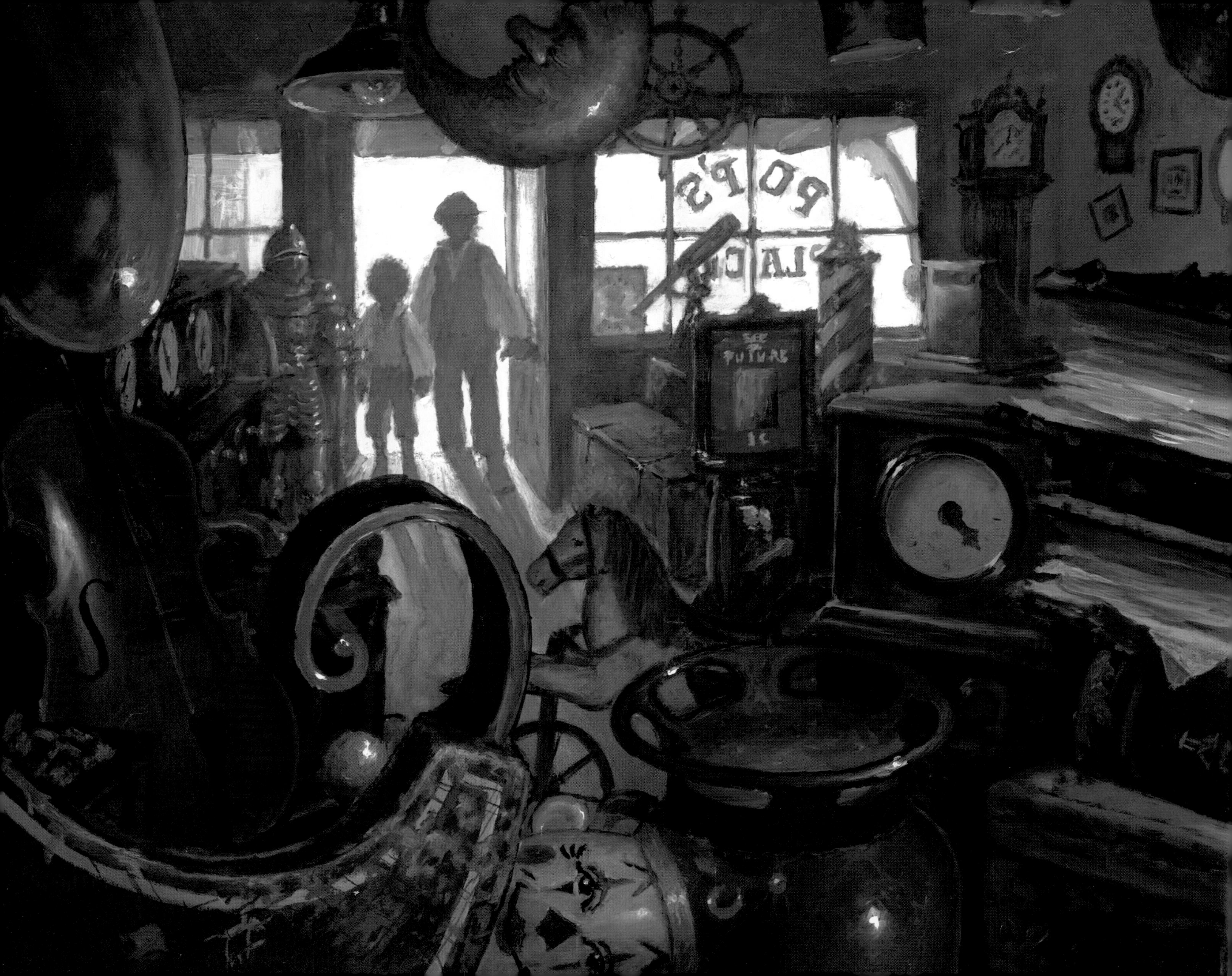
POP'S

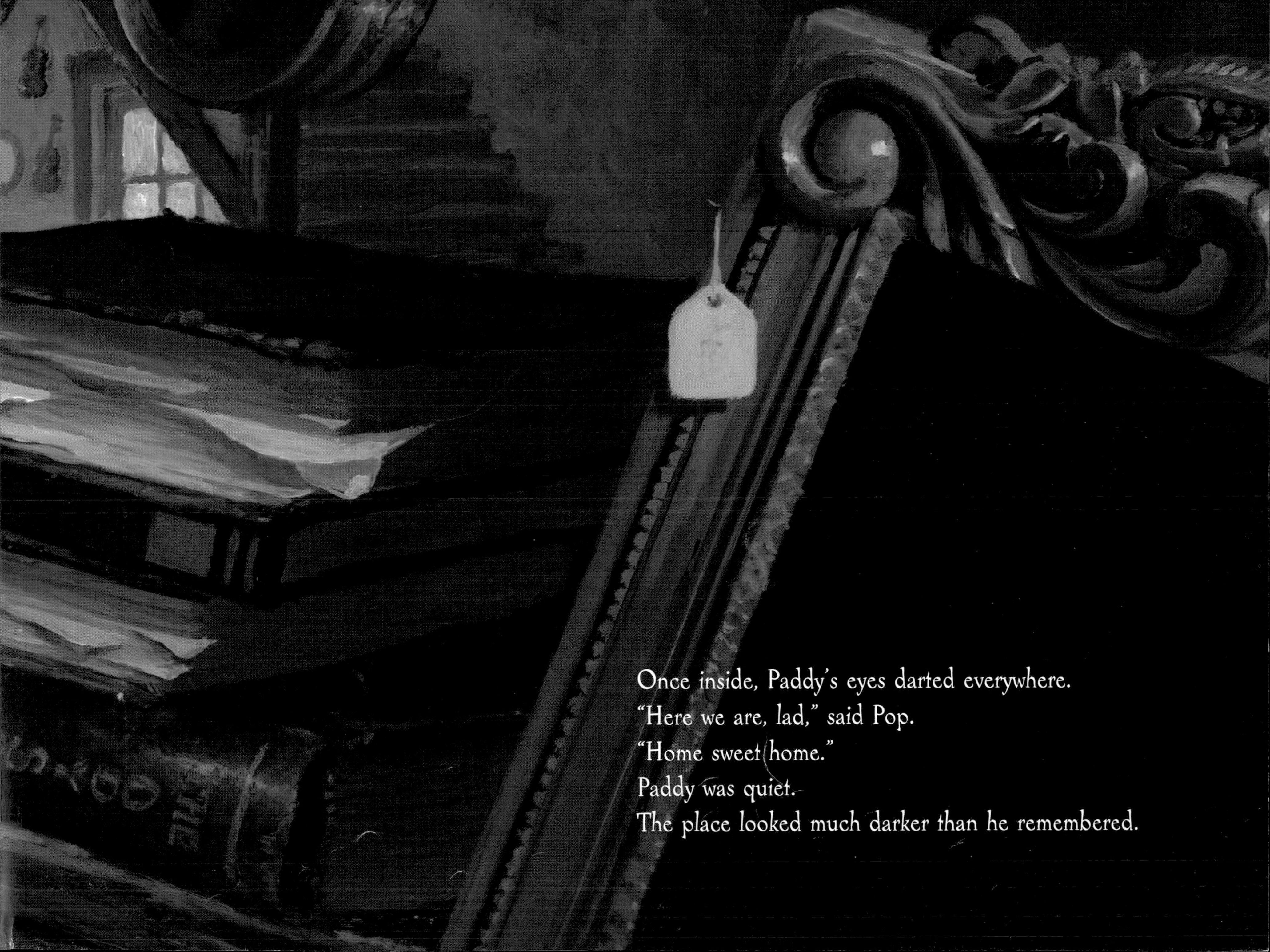

Once inside, Paddy's eyes darted everywhere.
"Here we are, lad," said Pop.
"Home sweet home."
Paddy was quiet.
The place looked much darker than he remembered.

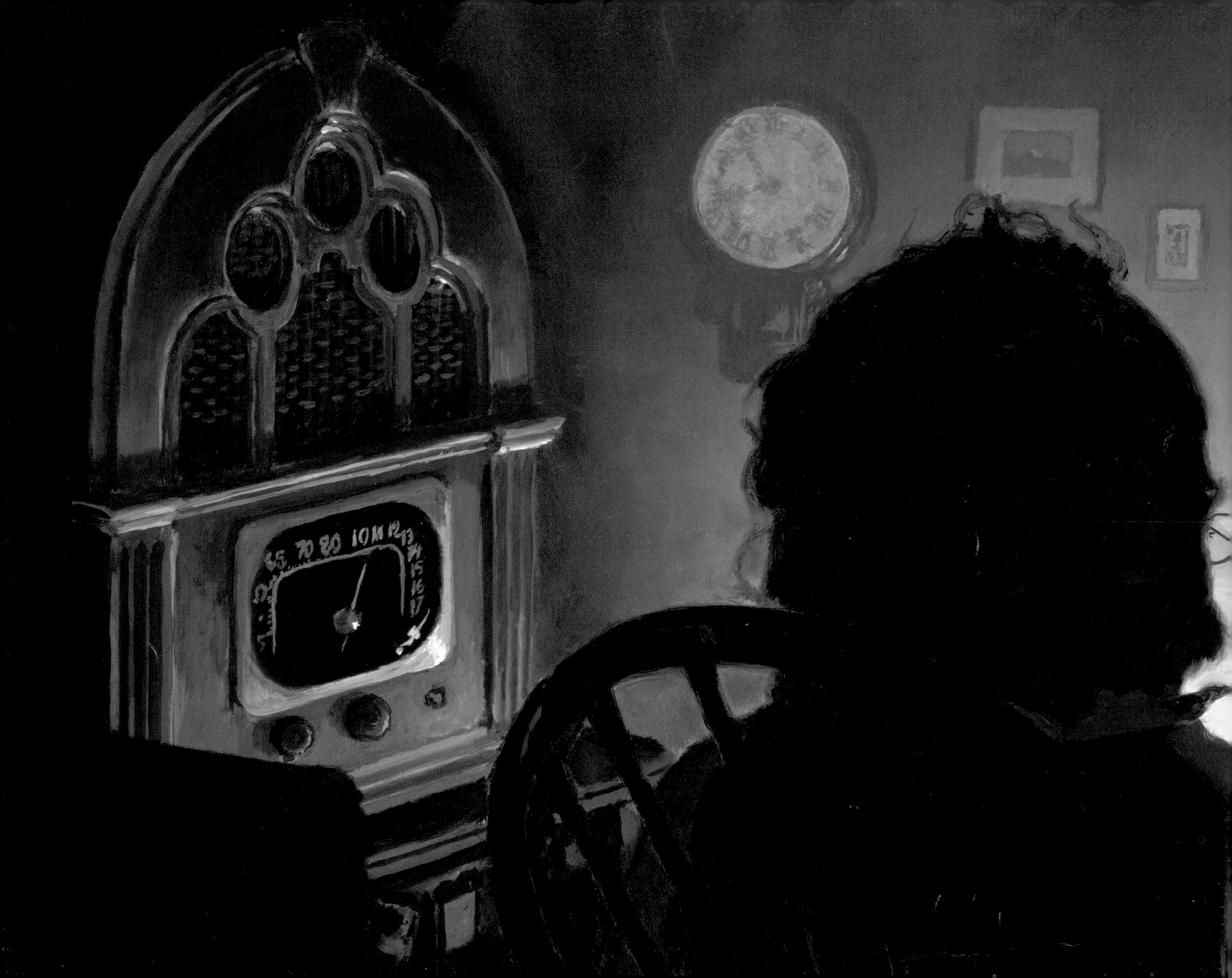

That night after supper Paddy and Pop listened to the radio.
"Good evening," said the announcer in a deep voice,
"and welcome to Monster Radio Theater."
Paddy inched closer to Pop's side.
"In tonight's tale, a young fellow is lost in a mansion
lit only by the moon and one flickering candle."

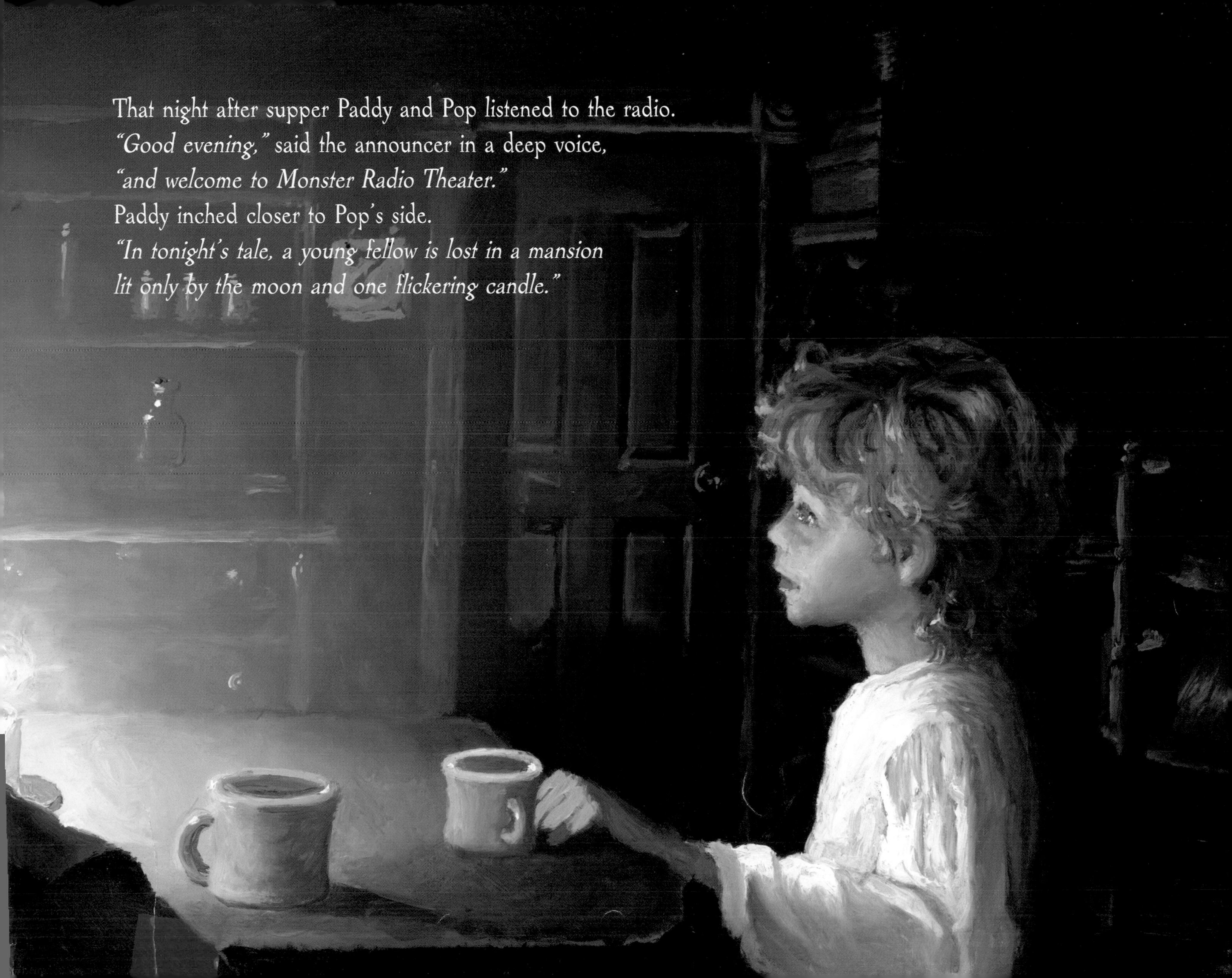

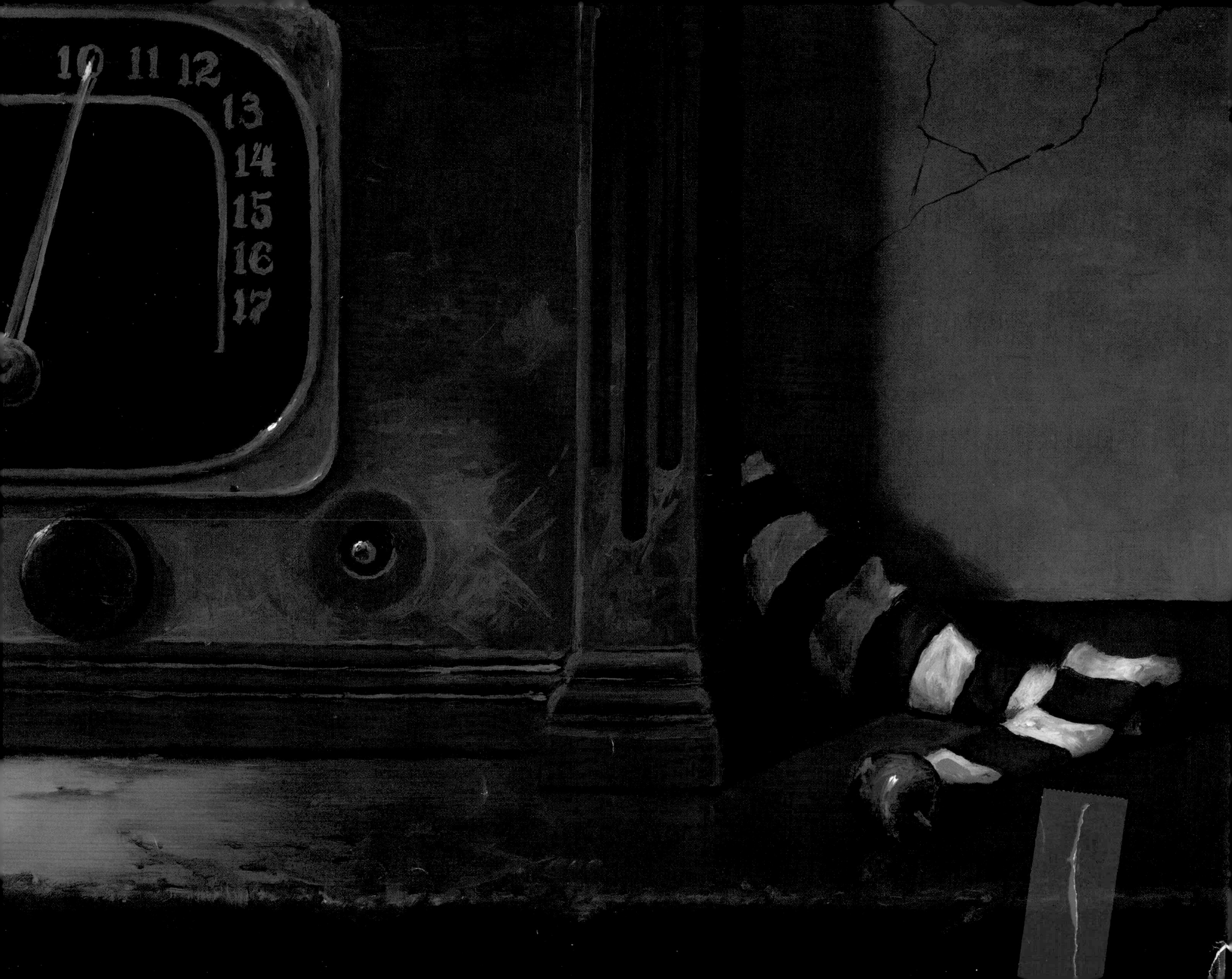
10 11 12
13
14
15
16
17

Later, at bedtime, Paddy was afraid.

"Pop!" he said. "I think I hear the monster from the radio."

"Don't you worry," said Pop. "That was just a story.
There are no real monsters."

Paddy wasn't so sure.

"That's what the monsters want you to think," he said.

He tried to sleep,
but the creaks and cracking sounds wouldn't let him.

Finally, he woke up Pop.

"I hear a monster," he said. "I just know it."

Pop was quiet for a moment.

"Hang on," he said. "I'll be right back."

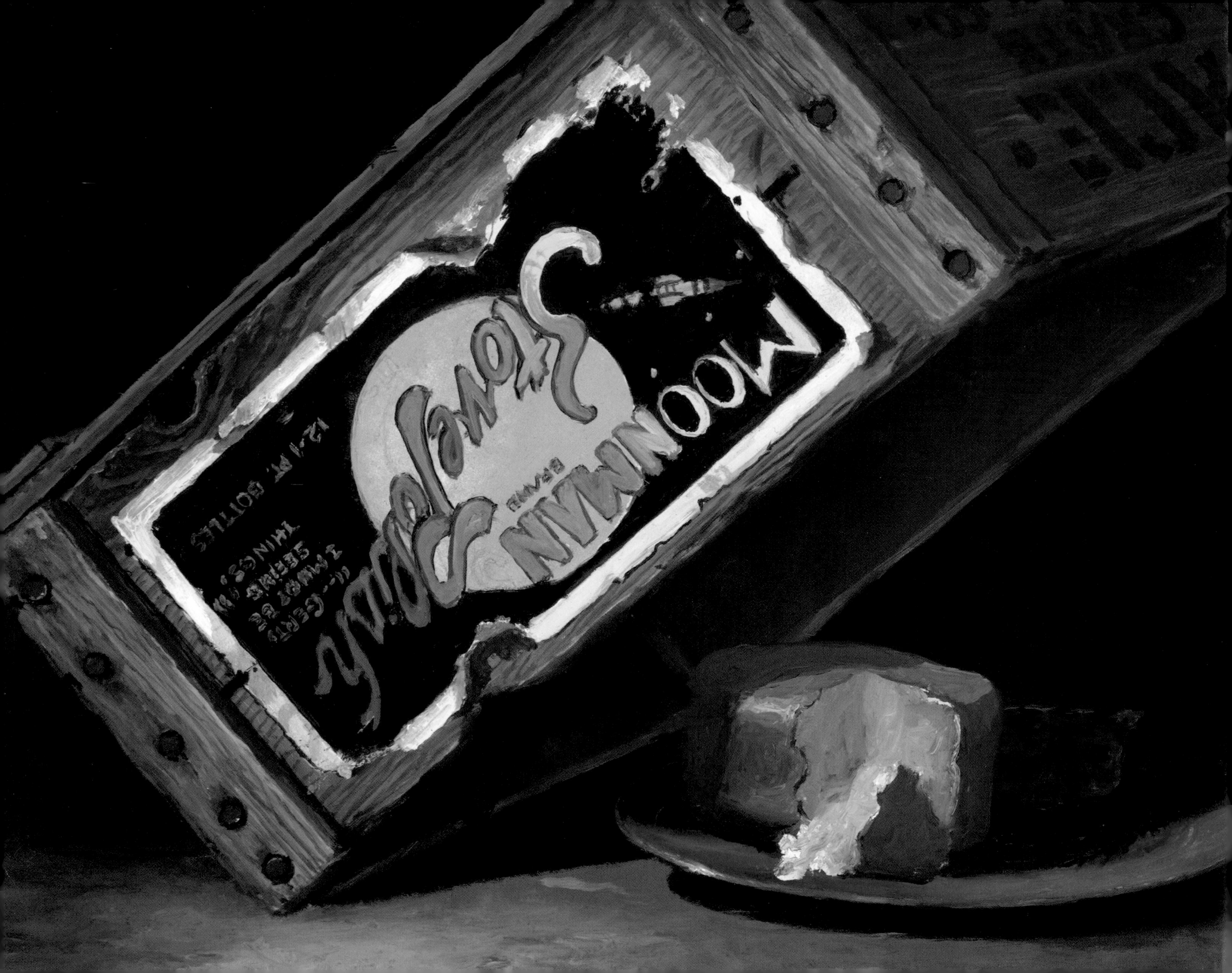
MOONMAN
BRAND
12-1 PT. BOTTLES

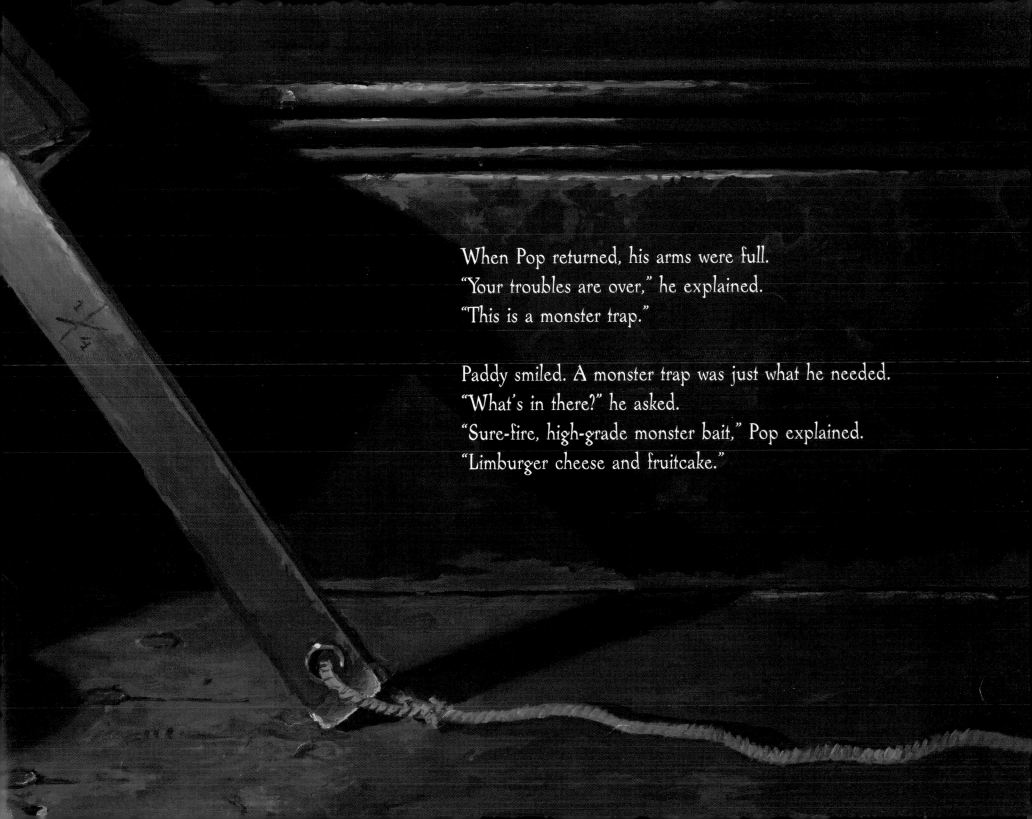

When Pop returned, his arms were full.
"Your troubles are over," he explained.
"This is a monster trap."

Paddy smiled. A monster trap was just what he needed.
"What's in there?" he asked.
"Sure-fire, high-grade monster bait," Pop explained.
"Limburger cheese and fruitcake."

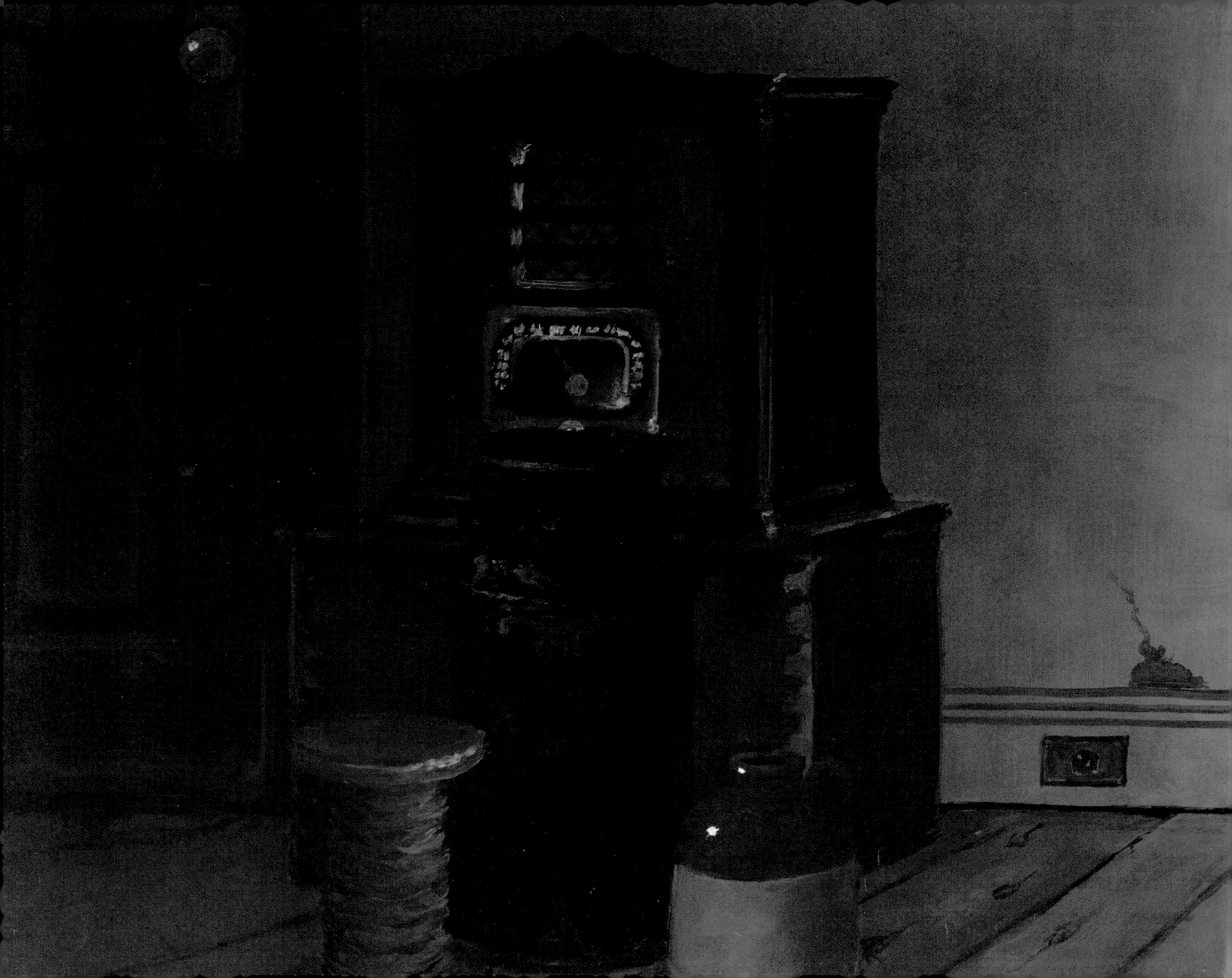

And sure enough, in the middle of the night,
something came out and took a good look around.

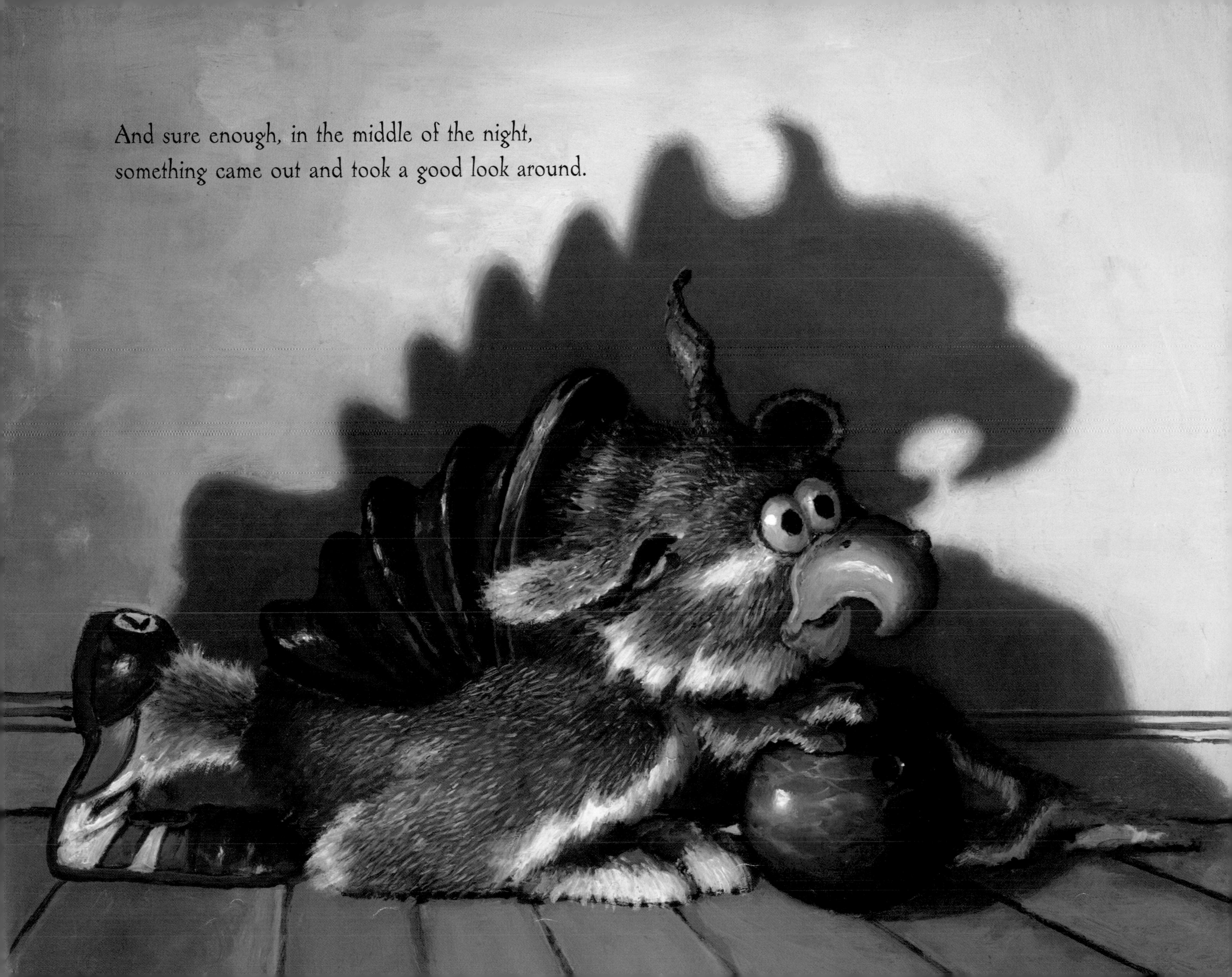

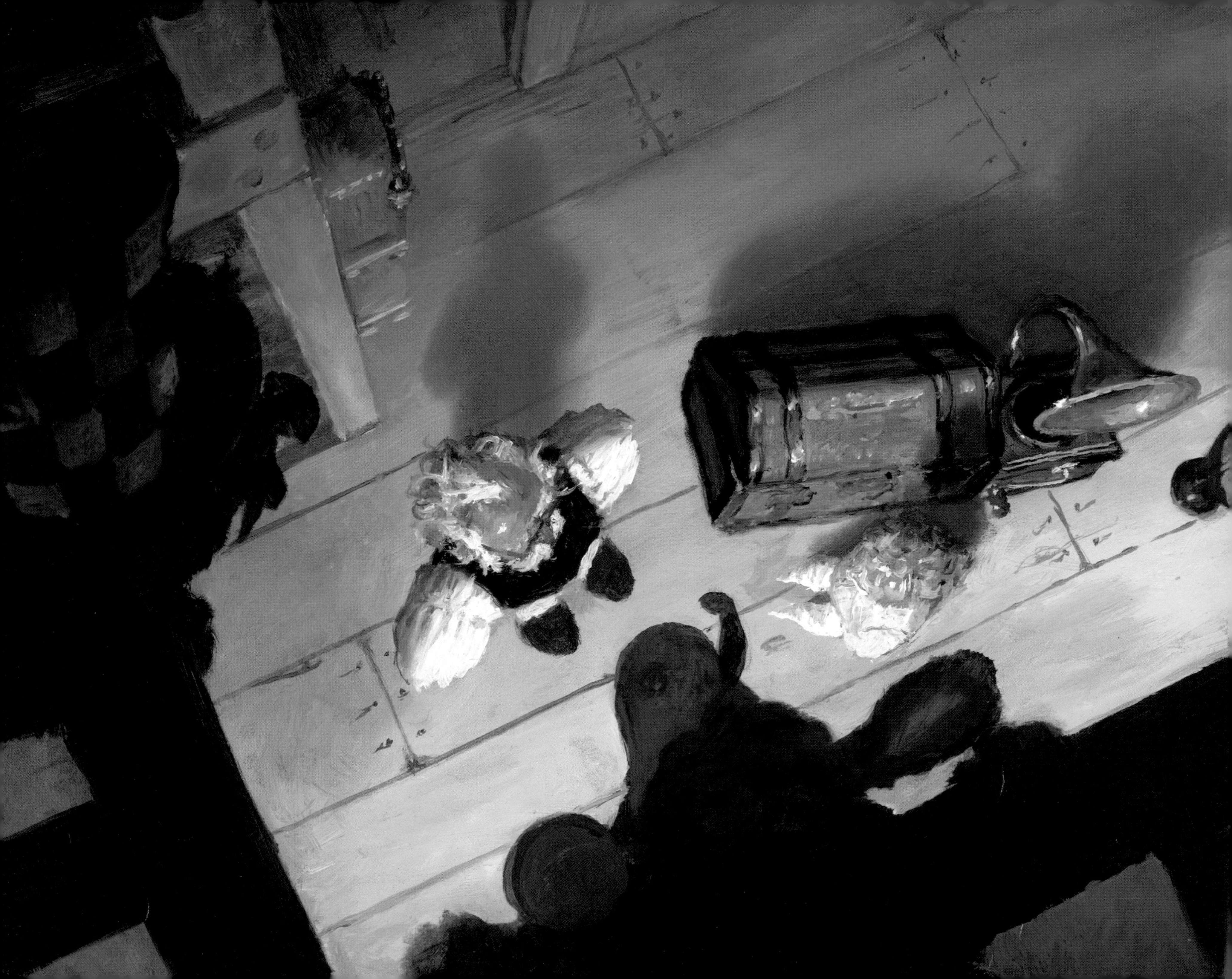

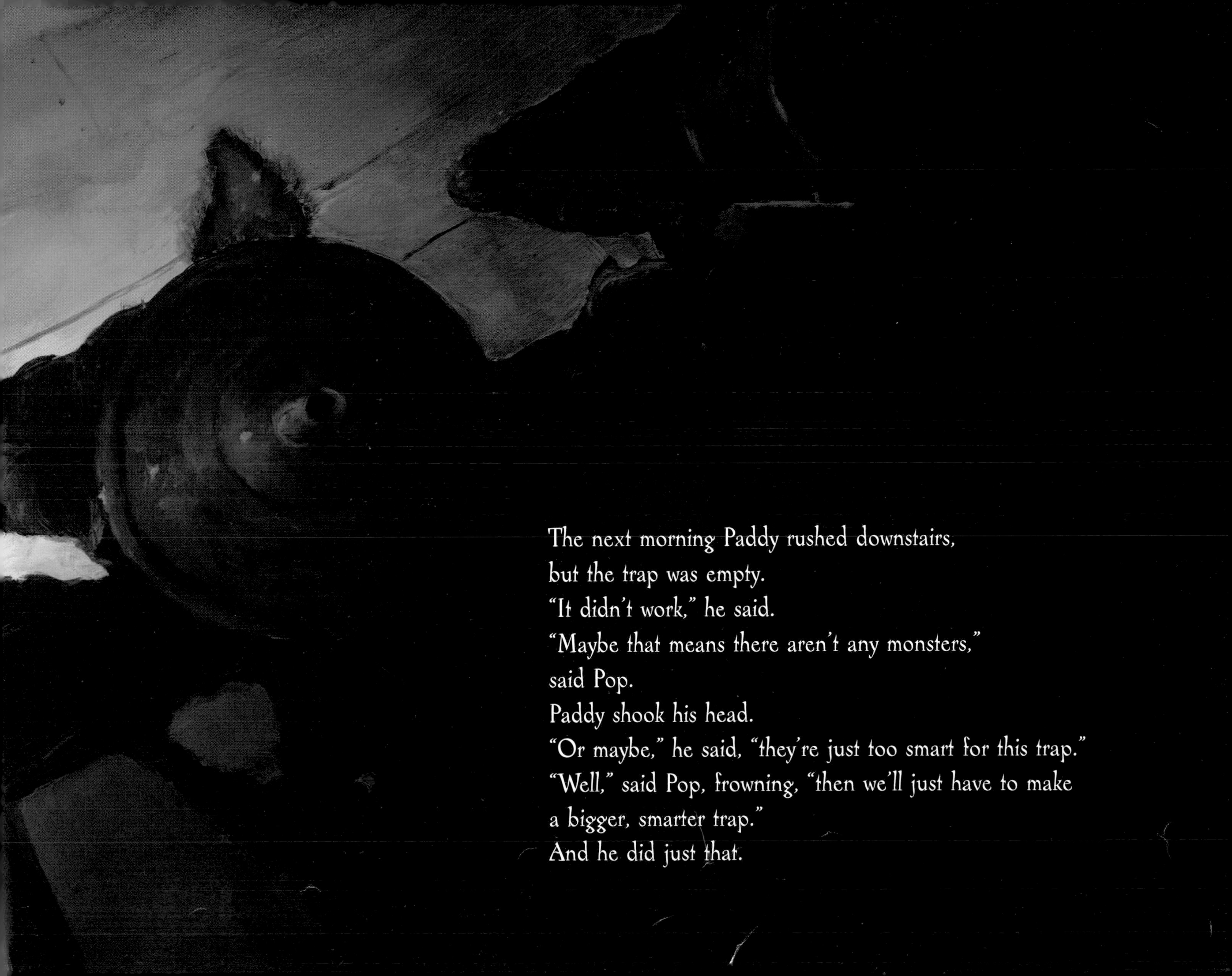

The next morning Paddy rushed downstairs,
but the trap was empty.
"It didn't work," he said.
"Maybe that means there aren't any monsters,"
said Pop.
Paddy shook his head.
"Or maybe," he said, "they're just too smart for this trap."
"Well," said Pop, frowning, "then we'll just have to make
a bigger, smarter trap."
And he did just that.

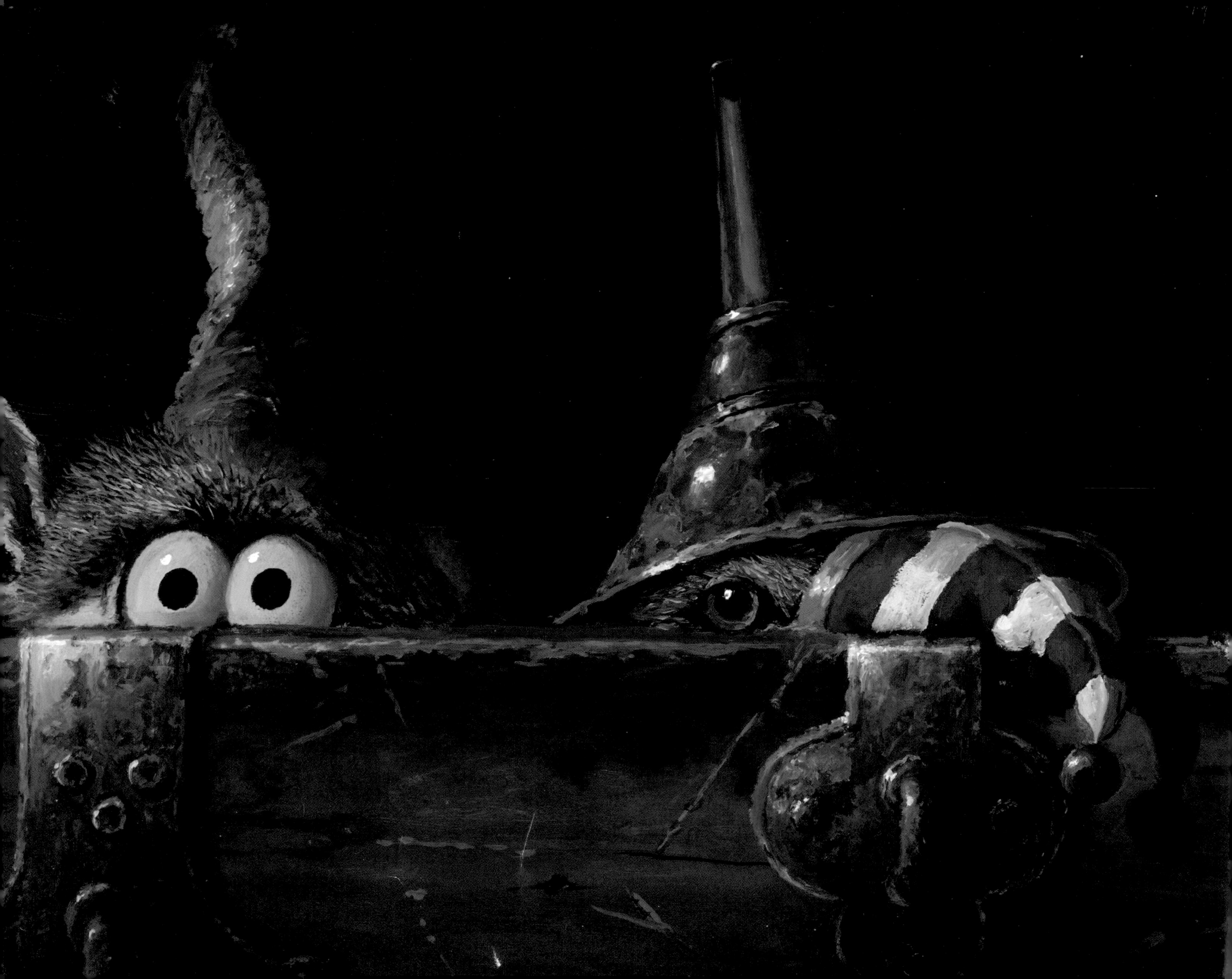

That night the first monster got some company.

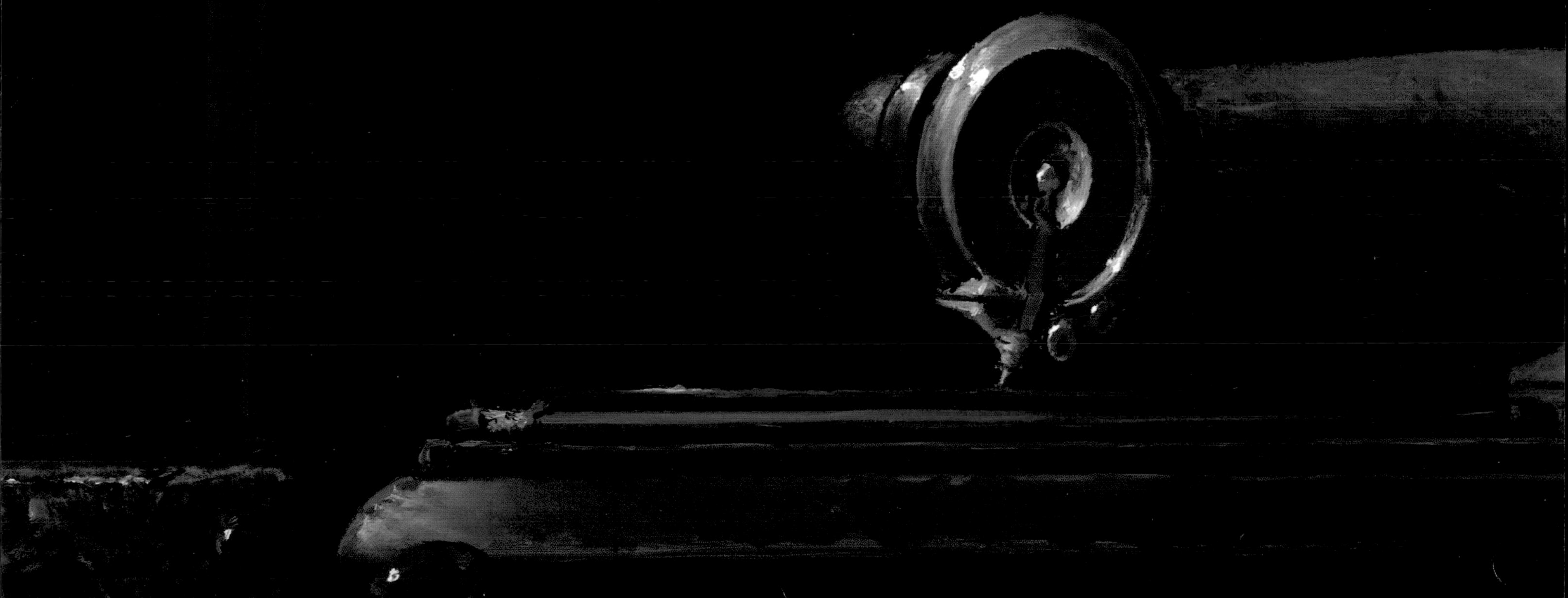

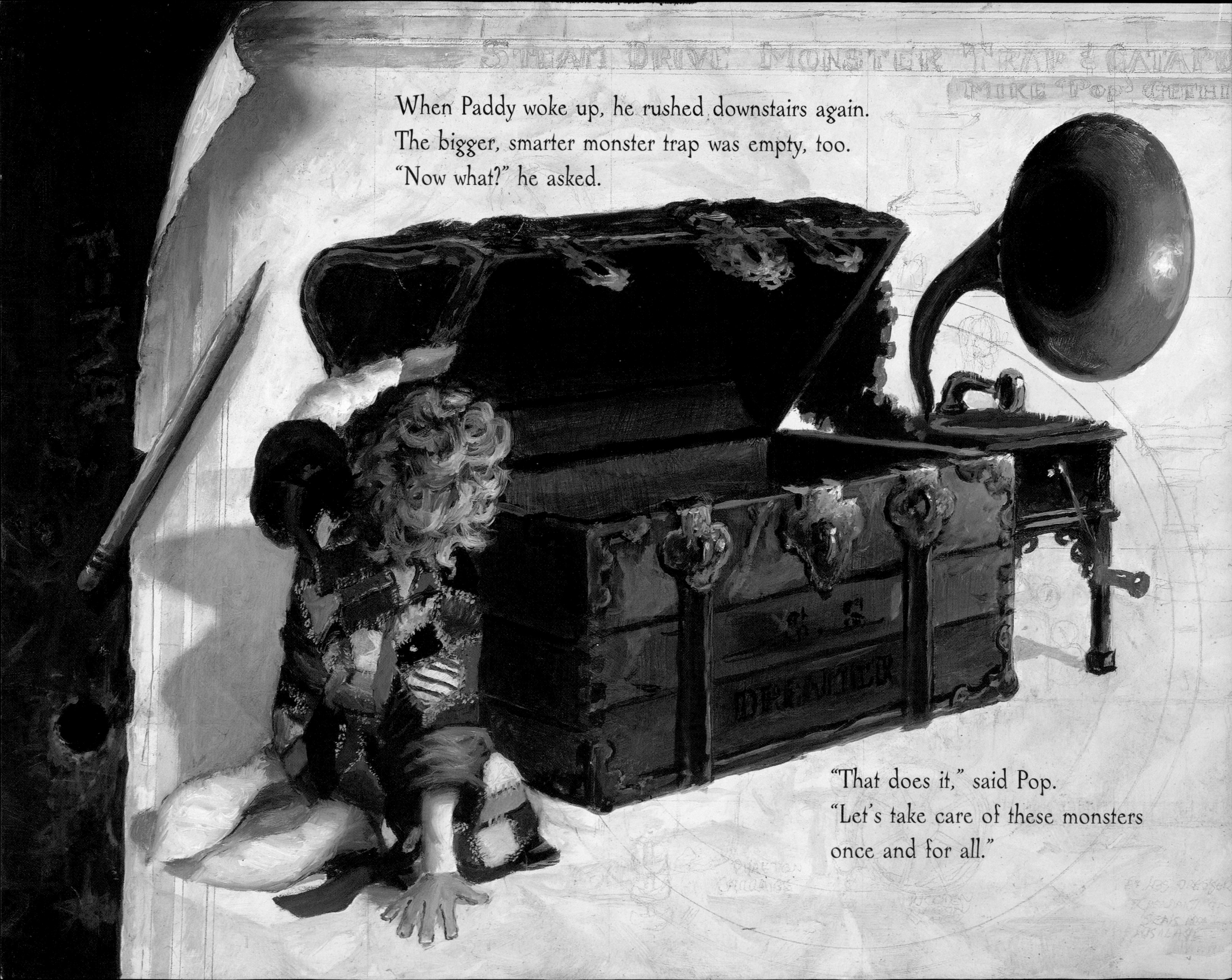
STEAM DRIVE MONSTER TRAP
DREAMER

When Paddy woke up, he rushed downstairs again. The bigger, smarter monster trap was empty, too. "Now what?" he asked.

"That does it," said Pop. "Let's take care of these monsters once and for all."

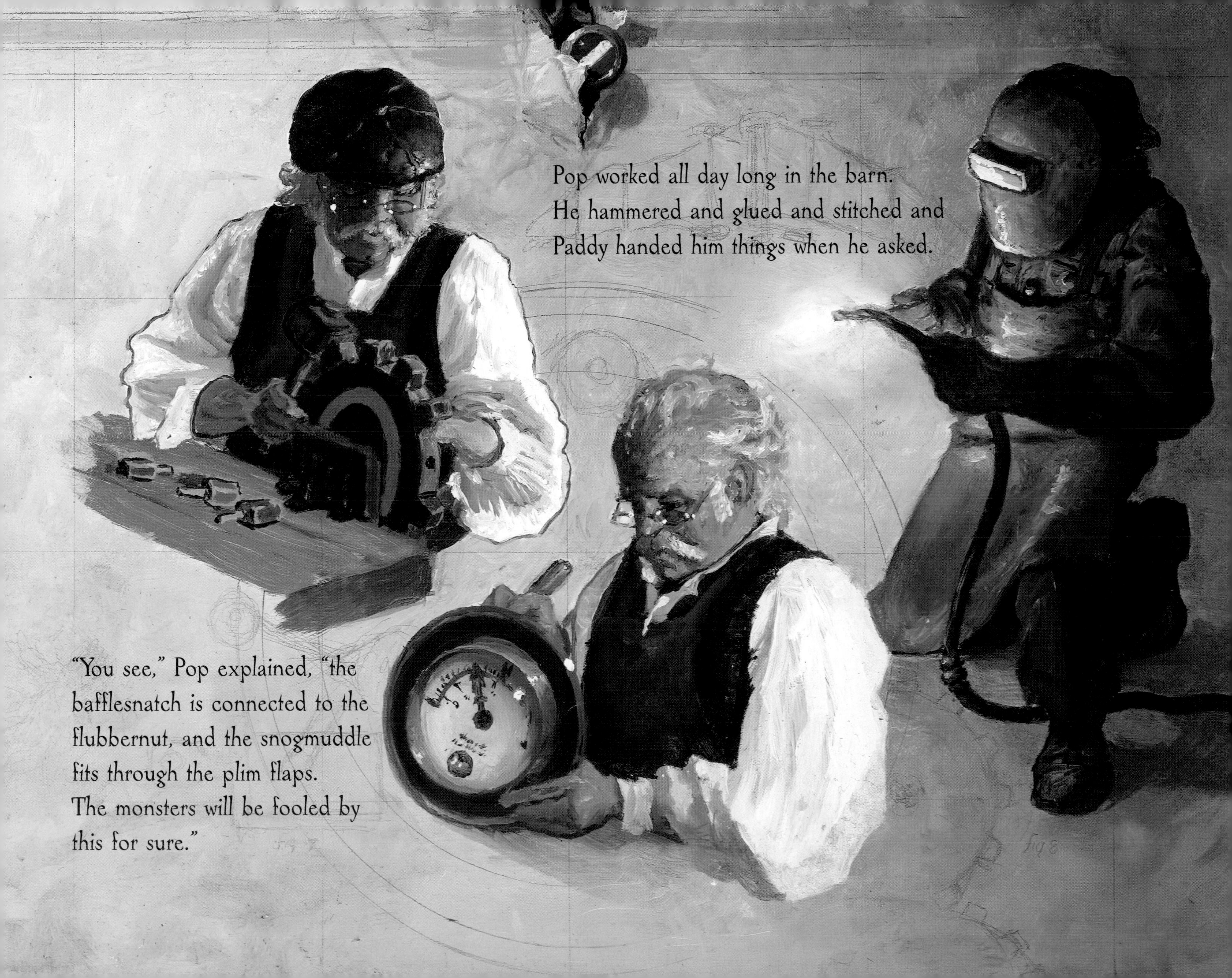

Pop worked all day long in the barn.
He hammered and glued and stitched and
Paddy handed him things when he asked.

"You see," Pop explained, "the
bafflesnatch is connected to the
flubbernut, and the snogmuddle
fits through the plim flaps.
The monsters will be fooled by
this for sure."

It was dark before everything was done.
"What do you think?" Pop asked Paddy.
Paddy took a long look.
"This will work," he said.
"It has to."

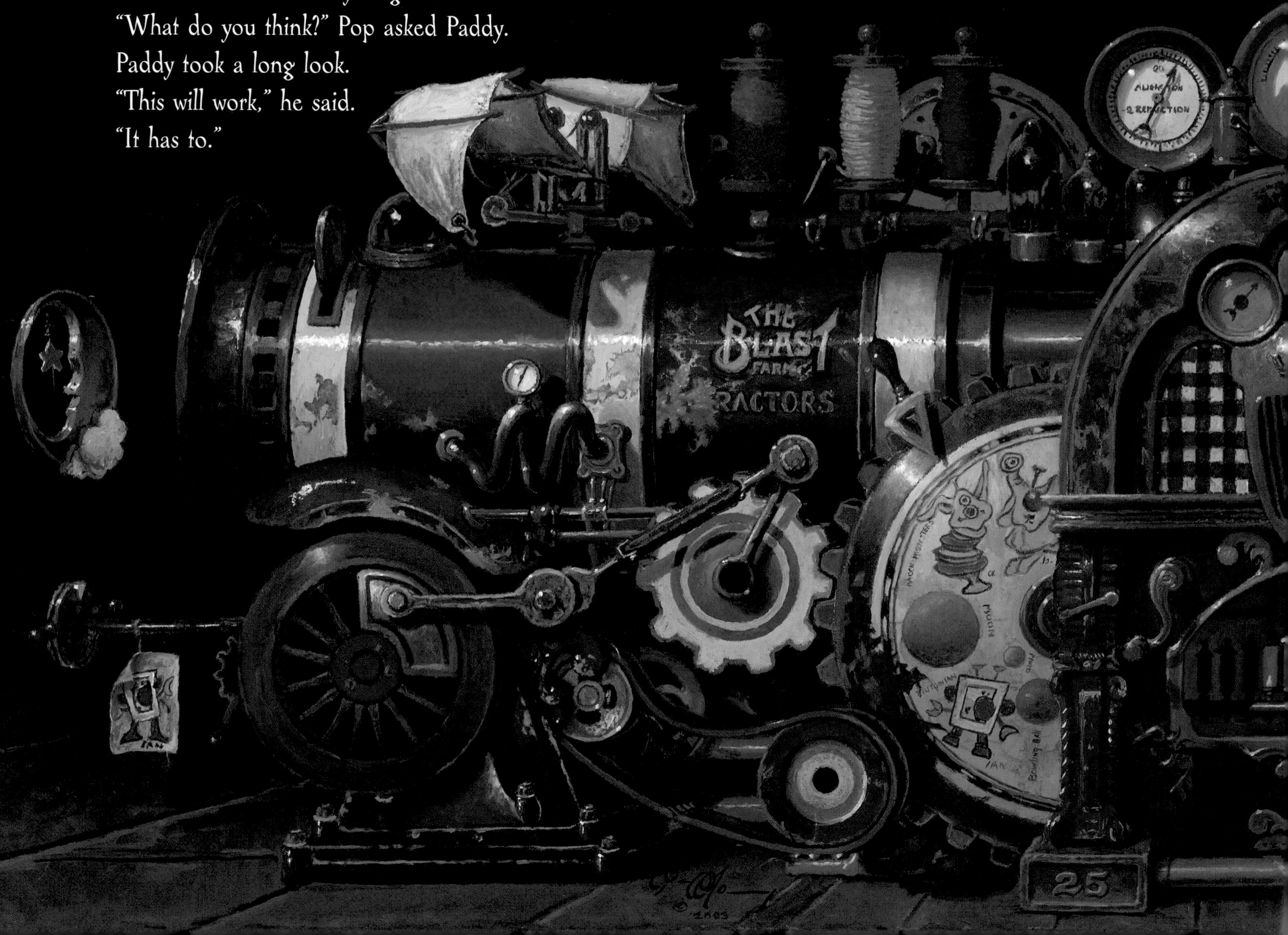
THE BLAST FARM
RACTORS
25

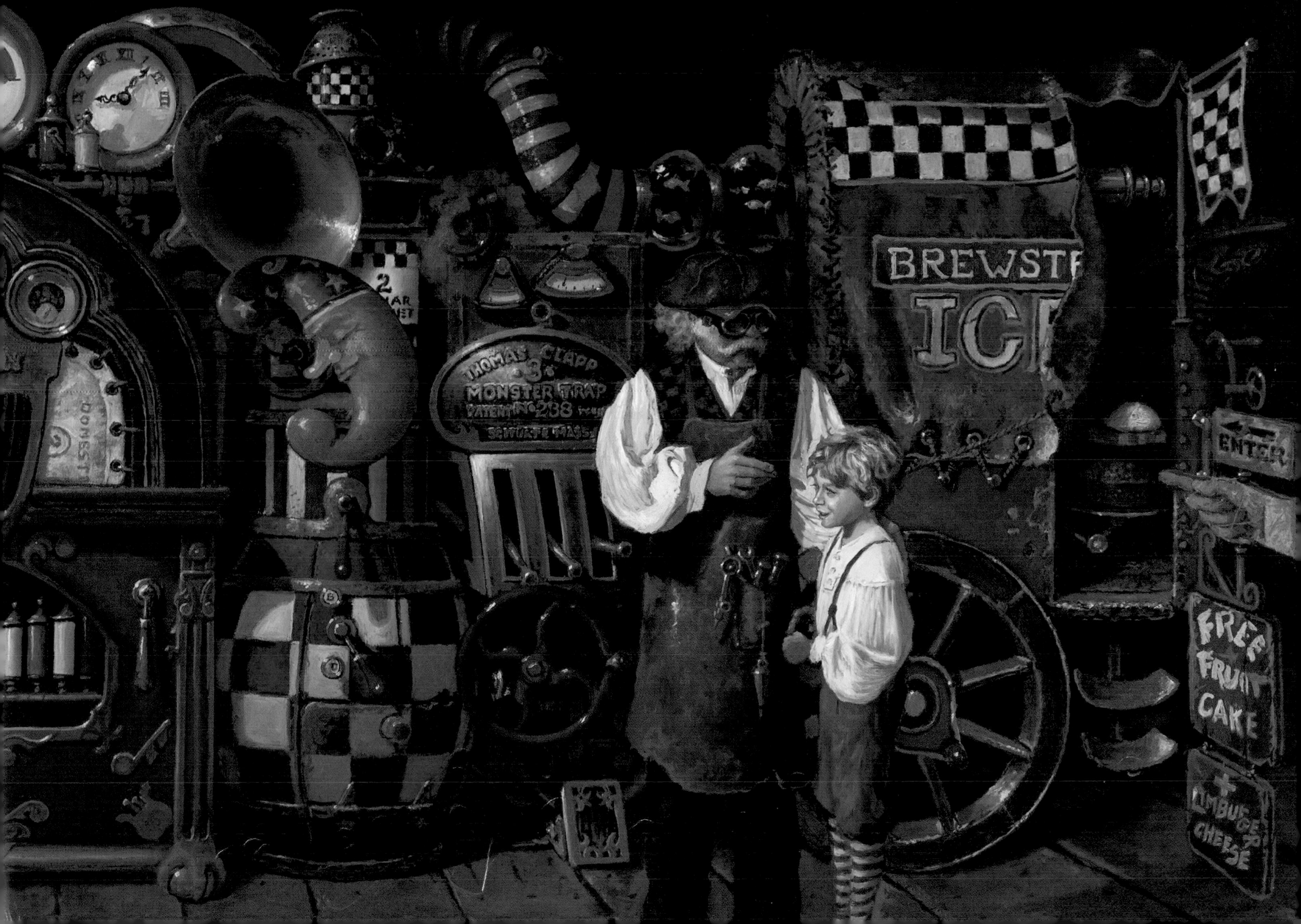
THOMAS CLAPP
MONSTER TRAP
PATENT NO. 238
SCITUATE MASS.
BREWST
ICE
ENTER
FREE FRUIT CAKE
+ LIMBURGER CHEESE

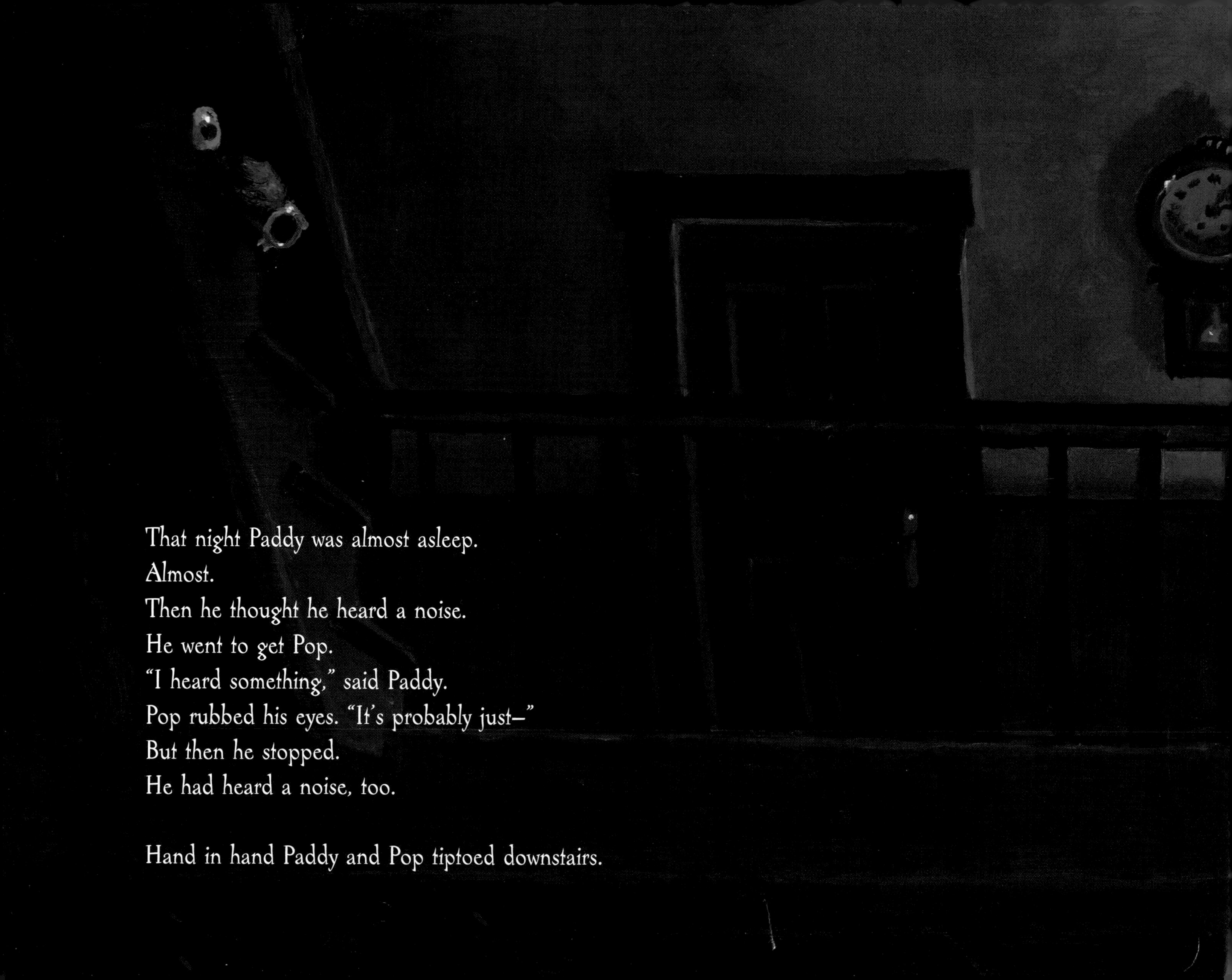

That night Paddy was almost asleep.
Almost.
Then he thought he heard a noise.
He went to get Pop.
"I heard something," said Paddy.
Pop rubbed his eyes. "It's probably just–"
But then he stopped.
He had heard a noise, too.

Hand in hand Paddy and Pop tiptoed downstairs.

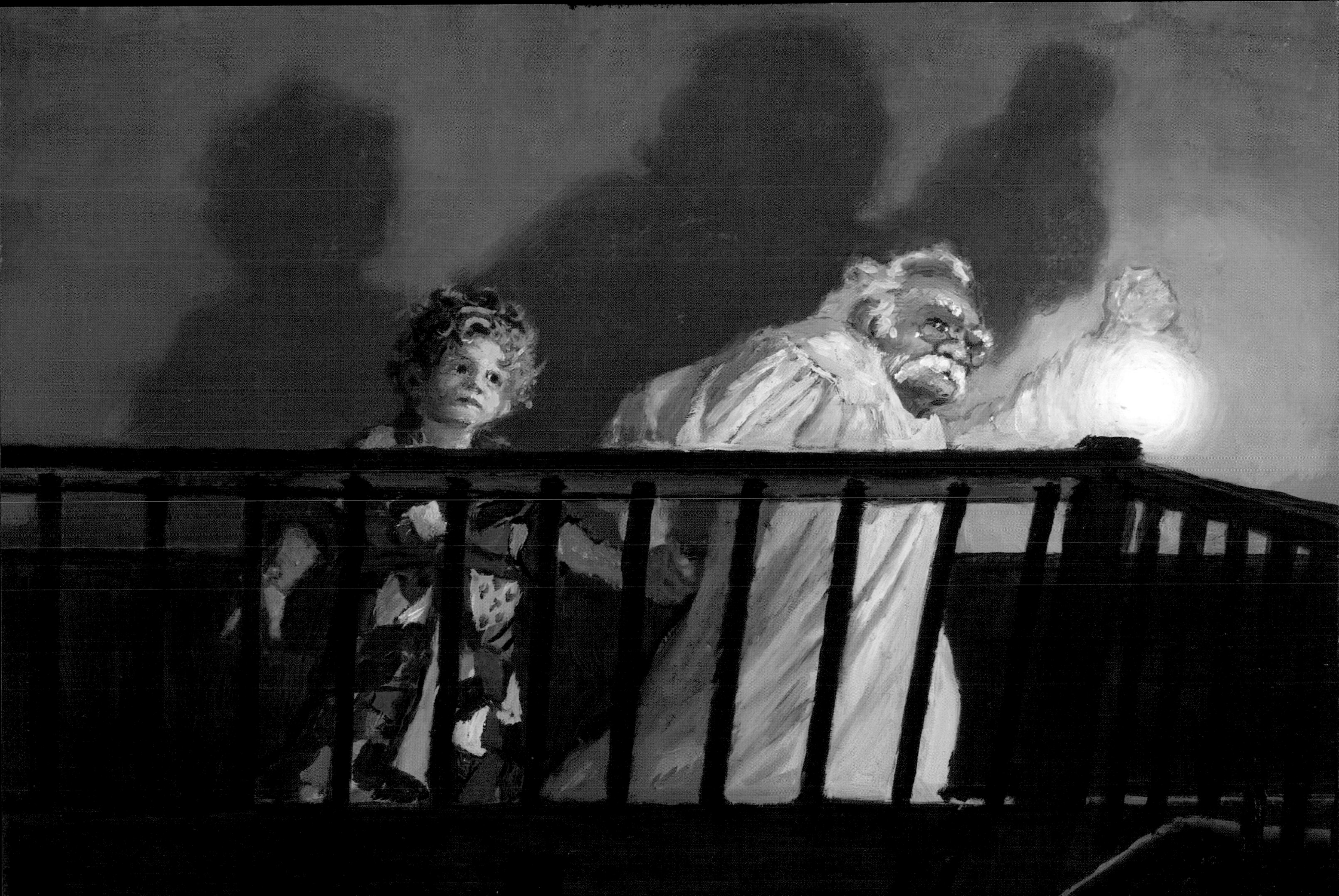

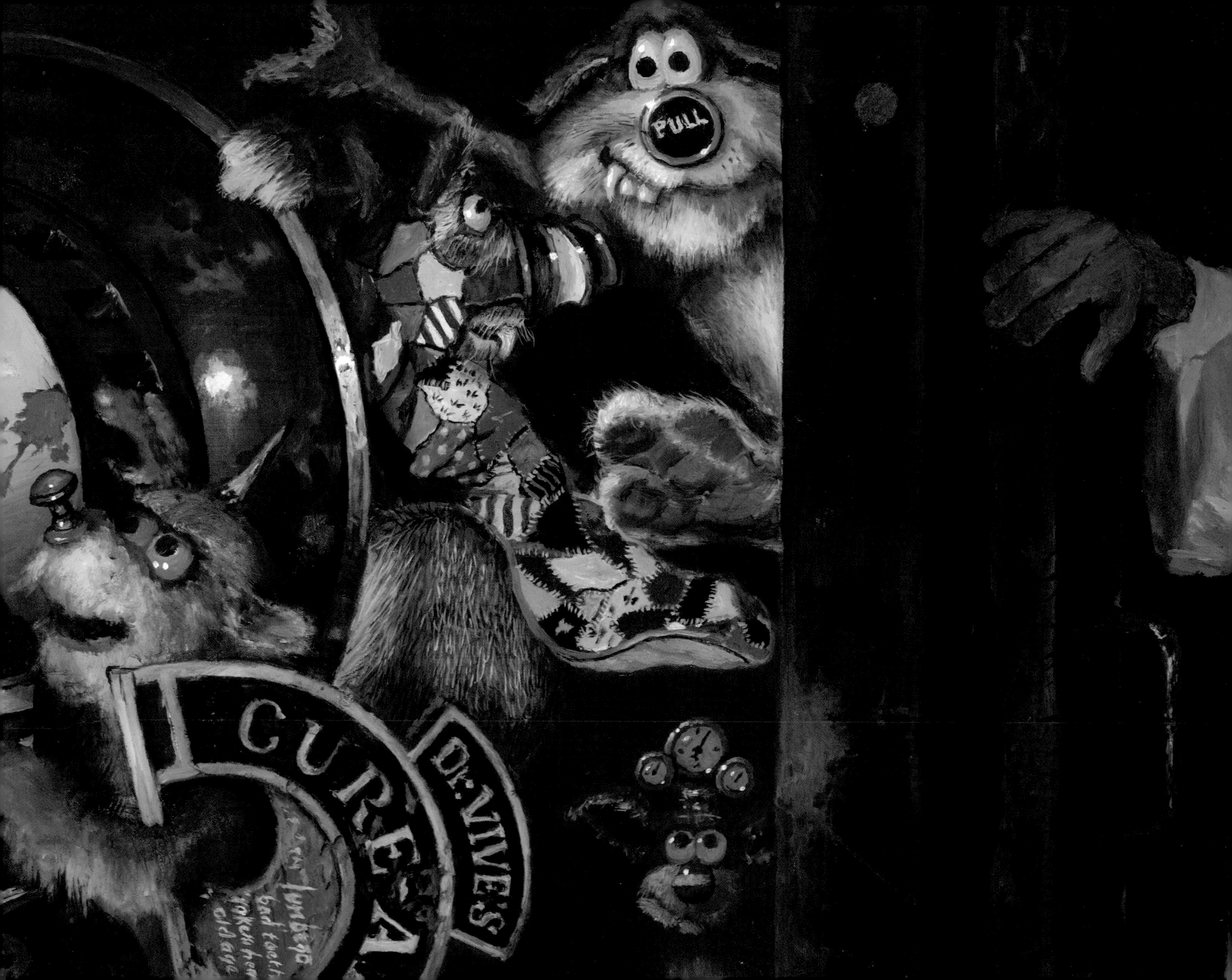
PULL
I
CURE
A
Dr. VIVE'S
lumbago
bad teeth
old age

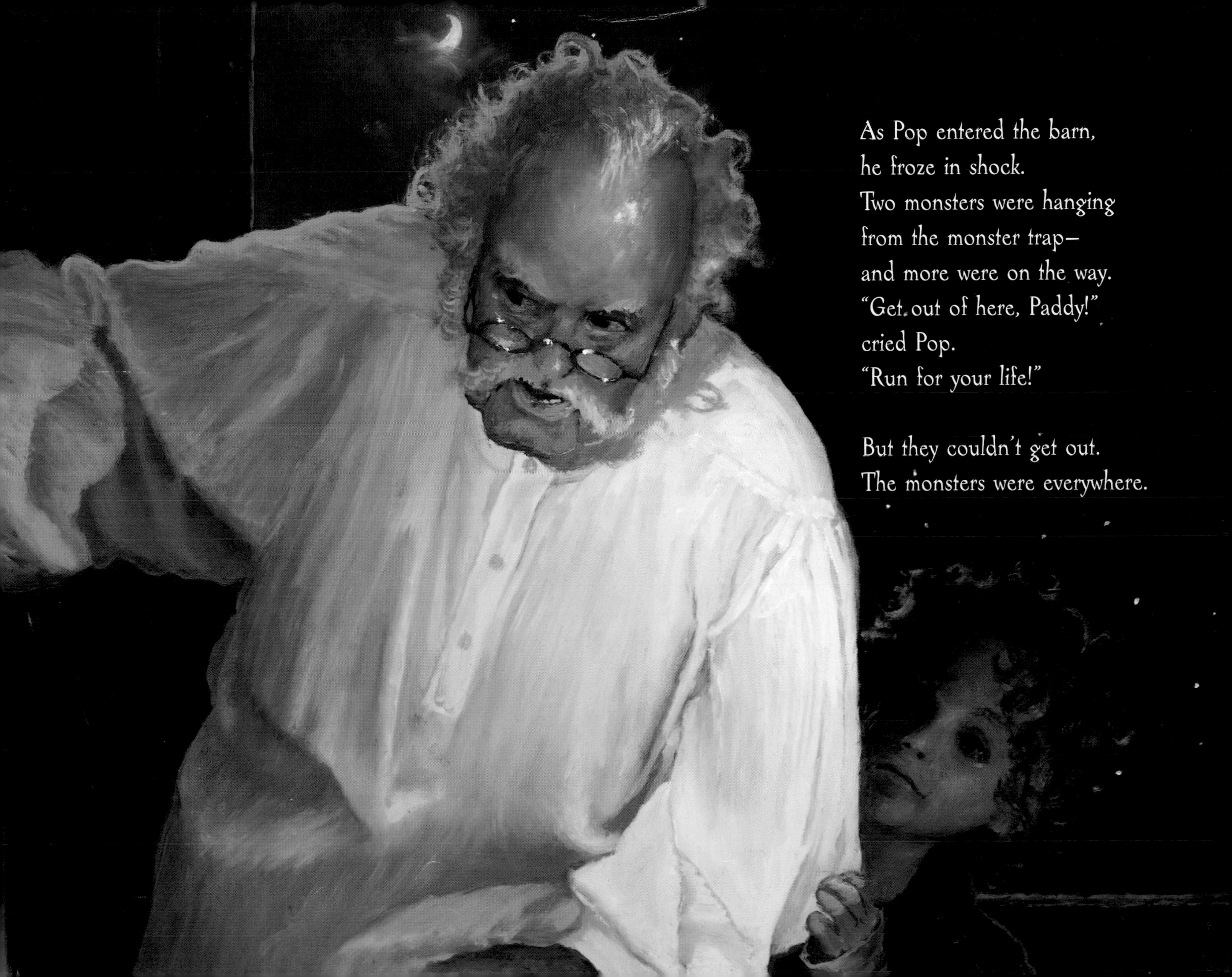

As Pop entered the barn,
he froze in shock.
Two monsters were hanging
from the monster trap—
and more were on the way.
"Get out of here, Paddy!"
cried Pop.
"Run for your life!"

But they couldn't get out.
The monsters were everywhere.

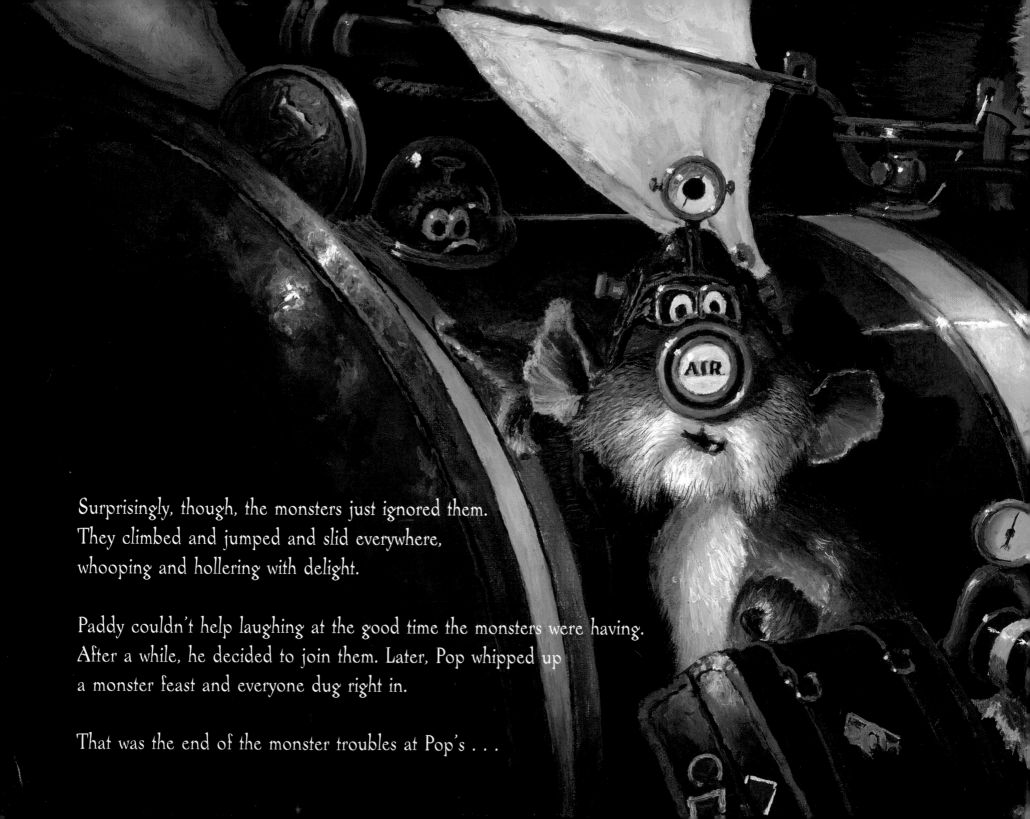

Surprisingly, though, the monsters just ignored them.
They climbed and jumped and slid everywhere,
whooping and hollering with delight.

Paddy couldn't help laughing at the good time the monsters were having.
After a while, he decided to join them. Later, Pop whipped up
a monster feast and everyone dug right in.

That was the end of the monster troubles at Pop's . . .

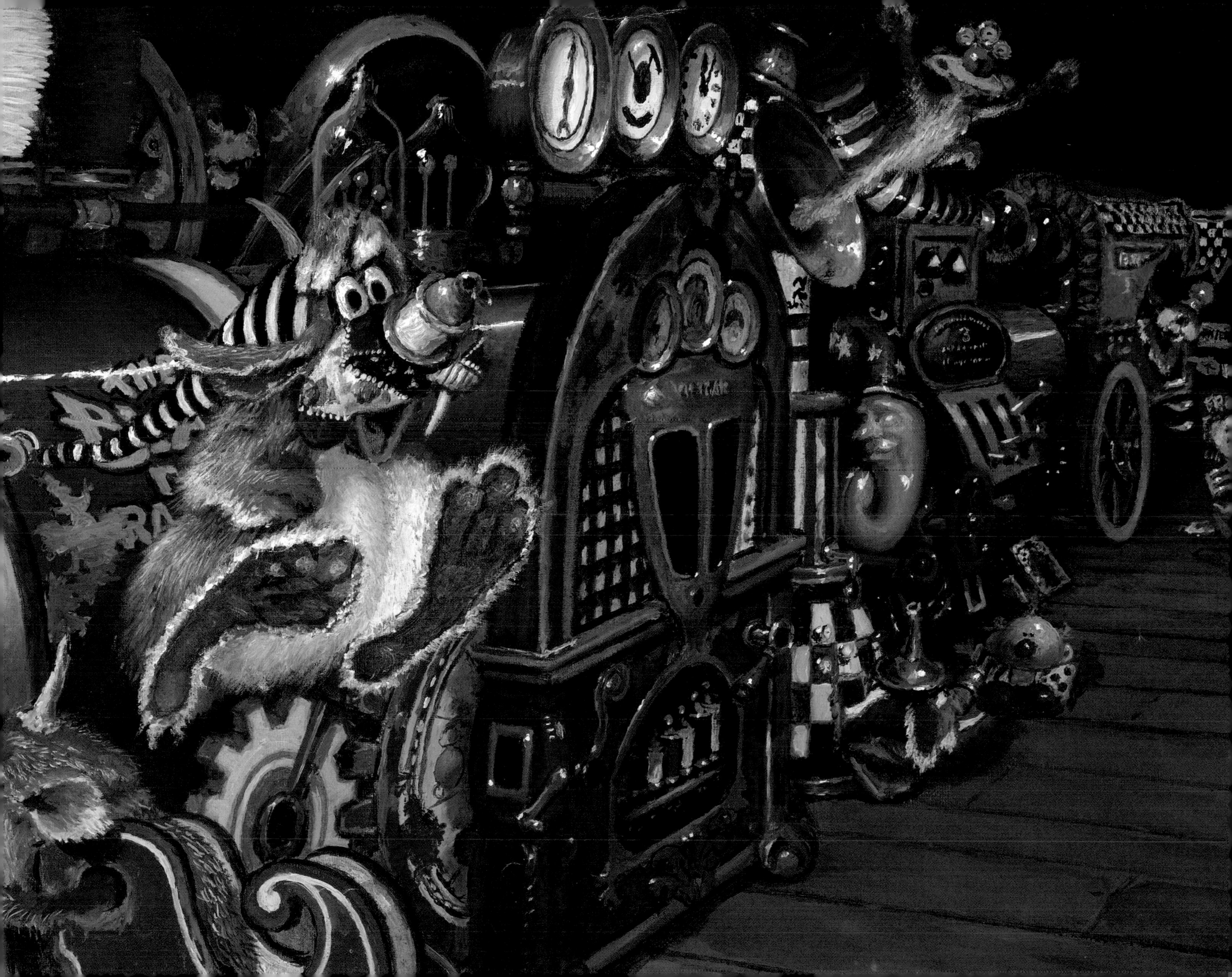

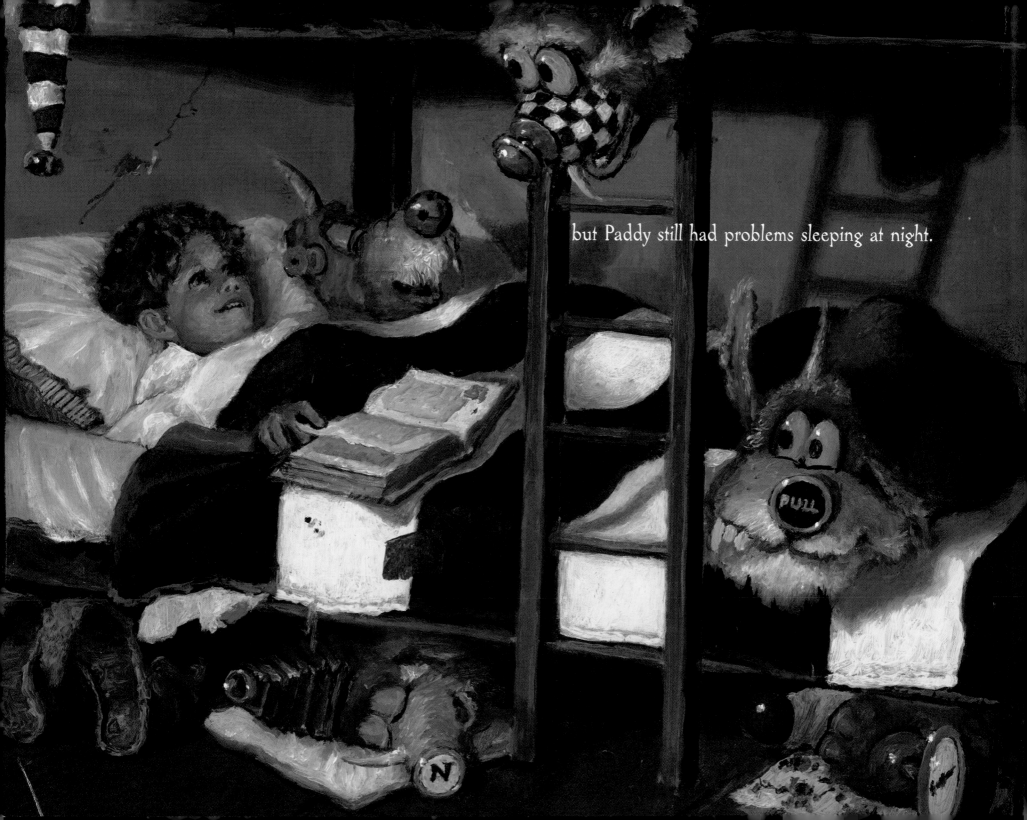

but Paddy still had problems sleeping at night.

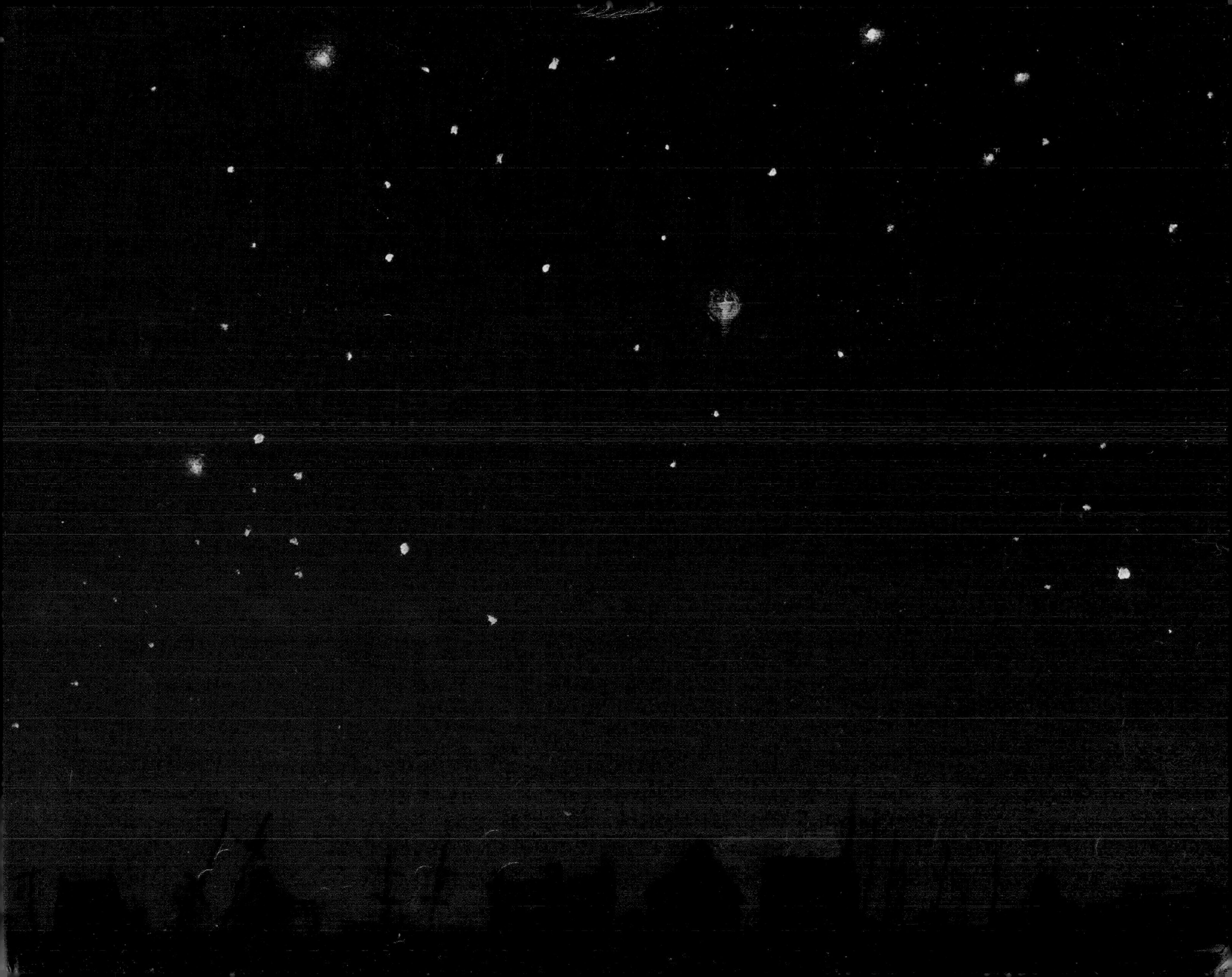

ACE
JUNK
YARD
GRANITE
2